OFF YOU GO

A MYSTERY NOVELLA

BENJAMIN BLACKMORE

SANDY RUN PRESS

ALSO BY BENJAMIN BLACKMORE

Once a Soldier

Lowcountry Punch

Writing as Boo Walker:

Red Mountain

Red Mountain Rising

Red Mountain Burning

A Marriage Well Done

An Unfinished Story

The Singing Trees

A Spanish Sunrise

Sandy Run Press

For Patty and Bert
Don't worry, I'll take care of her.

OFF YOU GO

Benjamin Blackmore

1

She'd been watching him for a while. First from the parking lot, then from near the stage, where an old Gullah man thumbed his way through the blues on a beat-up pawnshop acoustic. Despite the heat and humidity of late summer, the farmer's market in Mt. Pleasant on Coleman Boulevard was packed with natives and tourists alike, lined up to fill their bags with local produce and all things pickled, and to taste the saltwater taffy and the boiled and fried—yes, fried—peanuts, along with the homemade popsicles and whatever else in the growing variety of food-truck fare.

Dewey Moses fumbled for the pack of American Spirits next to the cash register and fired one up. He handed the man in front of him his change and thanked him.

"Next," he said, eyeing the woman who had been watching him. She was now fourth back in the line, holding a stack of Dewey's famous black heirloom tomatoes, Cherokee Purples. He worked his way through the cigarette and whittled down the line of people, throwing in two or three free jalapeños to anyone who spent more than twenty bucks.

He finally got to her—his curiosity sufficiently piqued.

"Afternoon, ma'am. That all for ya today?" He took the 'maters —as his grandpa, the man who taught him how to grow things, had called them—from her hands and gingerly placed them in a brown paper bag. If Dewey died today, they could spit on his grave for a multitude of reasons, but they'd have to remember what he could do in the garden, especially with his tomatoes. At least there was that.

"Are you Dewey Moses?" the woman asked. She had wise eyes that Dewey had seen in many women over the years, the kind of wisdom and strength you can only find in the eyes of a mother. Her brown hair appeared to be colored. Wrinkles of age creased her forehead; perhaps she was a grandmother. She had a figure that told him that she'd cooked her fair share of fried seafood and apple pies too. Not that Dewey was judging. He didn't do that. But he couldn't help but notice the littlest things about every person, every situation. It was a gift and a curse at the same time.

"You're not the IRS, are you?" he responded.

She furled her brow. "Of course not."

"FBI? CIA? DEA? DIA? PGA? NRA? MLS? NBA?"

"What in heaven's name are you talking about?"

He smiled genuinely. "Yes, I'm Dewey Moses." He removed his plaid fedora, bowed slightly, and took her hand. "And you, my dear?"

She blushed. "I'm Faye Callahan."

Dewey had been told all his life that he made great first impressions. Enough people had told him that that he believed it, and he attributed it to an early life lesson. His grandfather had taught him to love people, even strangers. *Despite their shortcomings and faults or opposite thoughts*, he'd said, *love them*. Dewey still thought that might have been the best piece of advice he'd ever received.

He gently squeezed her hand and said, "It's a pleasure. What can I do you for?"

She looked around and then whispered, "I hear you are good at getting to the bottom of things."

Dewey put his hat back on and looked around. "That'll be six bucks for the 'maters." He lowered his voice. "I'll throw my number in the bag. Call me in a couple of hours. Okay, Mrs. Callahan?"

She nodded and went on her way. Amazing how word spreads, he thought. Before long, he would need to hire help. And to think it had all started when his neighbor at the market asked him to find her son. He had stolen her car and run away, and she didn't want to call the cops. Using a parabolic dish, Dewey was able to listen in on a conversation in the teenager's high school parking lot. Two days later Dewey found the woman's son down in Key West.

At 2:00 p.m., Dewey packed up the vegetables he hadn't sold into the back of his long-bed truck. As he always did before starting the engine, he took a moment to look at the picture of his family next to the speedometer. His wife Erica and two daughters, Sonya and Elizabeth. With his shorter stature and his angular features—his somewhat sharp chin and nose—Dewey didn't consider himself to be the most attractive man in the world, but somehow, he'd landed the most beautiful woman he'd ever seen. Erica stole every show. Made every other woman stare. Thank God his daughters looked more like her!

That picture was the closest he'd been to them in a year and a half, and his heart broke because of that more and more every day. He thought he'd known pain in his life, but that wasn't the case at all. Nothing, including losing his sister to cancer, compared to what he was going through now.

He cruised back to his little place in the woods on John's Island with the window rolled down, chomping on an apple. Just as he was pulling into the driveway, his phone rang.

"Dewey, it's Faye. We talked—"

"Sure. I'm glad you called." He put the truck in Park and ran his hand through his blond beard. "What can I help you with?"

"I'd prefer to talk about it in person. Is that possible?"

"Of course, Mrs. Callahan."

"Please call me Faye."

"Faye, if it's not too much trouble, why don't you ride out to my place on John's Island?" Dewey gave her the address, and she said she'd be there in an hour.

SHE WAS RIGHT ON TIME. Dewey had unpacked the crates of vegetables and fixed a leak in his irrigation system out back, and now he was on the front porch in a rocking chair with a plate on his lap and tomato juice running down his chin from the glorious veggie sandwich he'd put together. He'd grown almost every ingredient: tomatoes, green and red peppers, basil, sprouts, onions, and greens. Then he'd topped it off with some homemade pickles, homemade jalapeño hot sauce, and mustard and Vegenaise, all in between two pieces of fresh cracked wheat bread he'd traded for back at the market.

He took one last bite and set the plate down on the little table. Then he stood and lit up a Spirit with a match.

"Please come up," he said, as she stepped out of her BMW convertible, eyeing his property.

Dewey didn't have much left but the cabin and his instruments. Erica had kicked him out of their house, and she'd taken the girls. But he didn't blame her a bit. In a few days, he'd be one year sober, but before that, his sister's untimely death had sent him on a three-year binge as a full-blown vodkaholic. Put it this way...Bloody Marys had been his way of getting nutrients; vodka and water his way of hydrating.

One thing that gave him some sense of relief was that he had never been a mean or violent drunk. He'd never screamed at his girls or anything of the kind. Though it was certainly nothing to be proud of, he had been more of a funny drunk, embarrassing himself to no end. There was the time he flipped his riding lawn mower after too many beers. The time he woke up the neighborhood doing his best Pavarotti impression in his underwear. And the time he stood up on a plane to New York and tried to lead the passengers in a rendition of "Ramblin' Man" by The Allman Brothers Band. All embarrassing...but no one had gotten hurt.

Now, none of those stupidities were funny at all, and the only thing that mattered in his world was getting his family back. The divorce wasn't final, so he still had hope. He was a changed man, and with all the work he'd put into himself, he thought he deserved a second chance. He loved Erica and the girls more and more every day, and he'd never give up.

He'd been forced to leave their house over in James Island and make permanent residence in their cabin on John's Island one bridge away. The one-story log cabin was right in the middle of their five acres, three miles from any other signs of life. Just the way they liked it. It was raised six feet off the ground and had a nice front porch, but there was a lot of work that needed to be done.

The best part about the property was the fertile soil. The land had never been farmed before and was chock full of good nutrients. He could grow cucumbers longer than your arm and jalapeños that could melt your wrinkles.

Along with ditching the Russian firewater, he had adapted a new lifestyle that had made an enormous difference. It was one that his wife had been trying to convert him to since they'd met at the College of Charleston. Organic tea instead of coffee.

Cauliflower instead of steak. Yoga instead of long, worthless conversations at the Crabshack that would not be remembered the next day by either him or the strangers he'd been talking to. He'd even traded in pesticides for an organic approach in the garden. The only thing he had no intention of shaking were his smokes. He'd switched from Marlboro Reds to American Spirit Lights, but that was as far as he planned to go. For now, at least. He had to hold onto something from his past, almost like he needed a reminder. He'd lost twenty pounds and gotten back to his college weight, and despite the cigarettes, he ran three miles four days a week. Not bad for a guy staring forty in the face.

He offered Faye a hand as she made her way up the steps to the porch, but she waved him off and used the rail instead.

"I like your shoes," she said. "They're...happy."

"Thank you." She was referring to his red Converse All-Stars. "I have them in every color. Today seemed like a red kind of day."

They both sat in rocking chairs and made small talk for a moment. He noticed the heft of her Southern accent. It wasn't the country-bumpkin kind, more like the haughty I'm-sixth-genera-tion-Charleston kind. She held the "Char" in Charleston long enough for Dewey to blow a smoke ring into the air and watch it rise. He loved hearing that accent; it reminded him of Pappy, his deceased grandfather, who had raised him from the age of three.

That porch offered a wonderfully peaceful view looking out into the Carolina woods. There were no signs of human distur-bance at all, just the grand old oaks dripping moss like honey and the hundreds of pine trees and the squirrels playing Tarzan amongst it all.

Dewey pushed back in his seat and said, "All right, Faye. Talk to me."

"My daughter jumped off the Cooper River Bridge four days ago." She stopped there, almost like that was all she had to say.

Dewey reached back into his memory. "Callahan...I remember

seeing your name in the *Post and Courier*." That was it; Dewey had a knack for remembering everything he had read. "Was it Gina?"

Faye nodded.

"I'm sorry," he said, looking into her eyes and really meaning it. He pinched his beard.

"Now, assuming you agree to help," said Faye, "I don't want you telling a soul what you're working on. My husband doesn't know I've come to see you, and I don't want him to. Some things are done better silently."

Dewey nodded. He'd also read about her husband, Hammond Callahan, who owned Brightside Development. Hammond had gotten some media attention over the past couple of months for his controversial efforts to develop Bird's Bay, a two-hundred-acre waterfront property right over the bridge from Charleston in Mt. Pleasant. Not too far from the farmer's market. At the moment, it was home to a World War II battleship, a high-end resort, a nature area with some of the best bird-watching in the state, and a very much-loved public golf course where fifty bucks could get you way more than your money's worth. It was the nature lovers and the golfers who didn't like what he was up to.

Dewey stayed on topic. "Didn't Gina leave a note in her car that she'd abandoned on the bridge?"

"She did, and people saw her jump. They ruled it a suicide." Faye's Southern accent kept getting stronger. "Even though they haven't found her body yet, I know they will. It took them two weeks to find the body of the boy who jumped last summer."

Dewey pushed away a vision of what the boy's body must have looked like after two weeks of getting picked apart by crabs. He'd read about that too.

"I'm not here because I believe she was murdered. I'm here because I want you to find out why she killed herself. Hammond doesn't want to know, but I do. I have to know."

"Why do you think she jumped?"

"I don't rightly know. I thought she was in a good place."

Dewey took a long drag. Faye was a good woman, and it made his eyes wet to think about how awful her world was at the moment. Parents didn't deserve to outlive their children. Dewey couldn't imagine losing his Elizabeth or Sonya. Yes, he needed the money, but he also felt compelled to help. Especially since he couldn't help himself. Discreetly wiping a forming tear, Dewey said, "I'd be happy to look into it."

2

Hammond Callahan gritted his teeth and pointed his finger at the man sitting across from him—the man the *Post and Courier* called his protégé, a moniker he had agreed with at one point. The offices of Brightside Development were off Broad Street in downtown Charleston, and the two men were in Hammond's high-ceilinged office on the second floor.

"Your incompetence," Hammond started, "is starting to outshine your abilities, to the point that I'm not sure what I saw in you in the first place. How the *hell* is it possible that your wife heard you talking to him on the phone? Didn't I say to keep the discussions off-line? Wasn't that the first thing I said? You got shit in your ears?"

"You did, but—"

"You are a worthless little bottom dweller and if there was anything I could do to cut you loose right now, you can bet your ass I would. But we've gone too far now. So I'm going to let you ride my coattails all the way through the deal, but if you screw this up, I'll be on you *heavy*. You and I both know I have every reason to be furious. My patience is wearing thin. You get your wife under control and make sure she keeps her mouth shut. And get the fuck out of my office!"

It looked like Rowe Tinsley wanted to say more, but he wisely held back, avoiding a punch in the face. Hammond stood with his palms planted on the desk. He watched Rowe walk out of his office and close the door.

Hammond took a deep breath and let his head fall. He couldn't lose the Bird's Bay deal. It was the culmination of everything he'd been working on, everything he'd learned his entire life. He and Faye would be set forever. A pile of money was right around the corner; he just had to keep everything together. What was left of it.

Of course, he could hardly ignore Gina's suicide; it would sculpt the rest of his life. Working these countless hours trying to push this development through was distracting him from the horrors of her death, but as soon as he let his mind slip into thinking about her—like he was right now—it all came crashing down.

His breath left him, and he collapsed back into his chair, his head in his hands. The tears fell, and he had to fight to keep from making too much noise as the crying came. He couldn't let anyone in the office see him in a state of weakness. *Never let them see you sweat.*

They were tears of anger and sadness. He hadn't been the best father. He hadn't treated her like he now wished he had. He regretted every time he'd raised his voice at his beautiful, innocent little girl. He regretted not being more patient with her as she struggled with her demons. He hated that the last time he'd seen her, he'd told her that she needed to settle down and get married, that Faye was ready for a granddaughter. He'd told her that so many times! He'd tried to *guilt* Gina into starting a family, when she hadn't even had someone to love.

Someone knocked on the door. "Hammond?" It was his secretary.

Hammond sat up and wiped the tears from his cheeks. "I'm on my cell. Give me five minutes."

3

Though it was Dewey's least favorite part, he discussed the monetary details with Faye. Since he'd been kicked out, he'd given nearly every dime he made to Erica, intent on making sure his family was taken care of. It was never enough.

As a dental assistant, Erica had always made better money than Dewey, but he still wanted to contribute. He had always spoiled his girls and wanted to continue doing so—which seemed absurd, considering he'd drunk his way into doing the opposite. Before he'd lost control, he'd been working at a plant nursery and singing in a local bluegrass band called The Carolina Lonely. Both had fired him the same month Erica had booted him. Now he was making a living off his vegetables and this little problem-solving business, which was finally starting to bear fruit.

Dewey gave a number, and Faye didn't even bother haggling. Dewey could only imagine how much the Callahans were worth.

"Let's back up now," Dewey said. "Tell me about your daughter." He'd found it best not to get too specific at first. Let her tell the story.

Her words came out in sadness, the length of some of the syllables pushing the story toward melodrama, though it most certainly was not. "Gina was twenty-eight, God rest her soul. She graduated from the College of Charleston five years ago, which was the extended program, as Hammond calls it. She took her sweet time graduating. I'm terrified that our spoiling her finally got the best of her. I have to blame myself. We never taught her how to fight. She didn't bother looking for a job after school, and the way Hammond continued to throw money at her, I don't think she had any intentions of ever worrying about it." Faye raised her hands and made a push motion. "But I don't mean to take anything away from her. She was a good girl, deep down. And she did have some drive. She loved working out...running, going to the gym and the rock-climbing wall. She took really good care of herself. But we just made it too easy for her. Her skin wasn't thick enough."

Faye reached into her purse and handed Dewey a photo. He studied it. Gina was sitting at a picnic table waving back at the camera with a smile that couldn't have been brighter. She had long red hair pulled into a ponytail, and tiny freckles dotted her cheeks. She was a stunning young woman—not exactly the "girl" that Faye kept referring to. Dewey figured a twenty-eight-year-old was as woman as you could get.

"I took this last week. Two days before. The red hair is her father's. Now, does this look like a girl who would jump off a bridge two days later?"

Dewey shook his head, but he was thinking how wrong she could be. People who kill themselves aren't always holding up signs that say *Suicidal*.

A woodpecker started going at one of the pine trees. Faye seemed not to notice.

Faye continued. "Now, she had seen her fair share of psychiatrists, and she'd been on and off every medicine behind the counter. I think that's one of the main reasons the police ruled it a suicide so quickly. But she was doing better."

"Hold on...now you're starting to sound like you don't think she committed suicide. With all due respect, you don't think I'm going to find your daughter alive, do you?"

"Of course not."

"And you don't think I'm going to find that she was murdered, do you?"

"I'm not sure. I don't think so."

"Fair enough. Long as you aren't thinking I'm a miracle worker. I am definitely not."

"No, I'm not expecting miracles. I'm simply saying that they ruled Gina's death a suicide within twenty-four hours, and it's because she had tendencies."

"Depression?"

"Sure. When she felt good, she was on top of the world. When she was down, though, she could be the devil. These mood swings could last months. Not bi-polar. She just had waves of good and bad. Needless to say, she wasn't the easiest child to raise. Like my daddy used to say, 'the fattest cow was hardest to corral.' I know we've always spoiled her, and we probably trained her to be who she was, but if she didn't get what she wanted, she would do her best to make us absolutely miserable." Faye sighed, exhausted by even thinking about it. "She'd been pretty stable for the past six months or so. It was one of those good streaks. I think she'd finally found a good combination of medicine, and our relationship was getting better and better."

"What medicine was she taking?"

"Zoloft."

Dewey was not a pharmacist but was familiar with Zoloft. He'd thought about taking it in the past year.

"Can you tell me about the night it happened? I know it's probably tough to think about."

She waved him off. "It's all I think about. A policeman woke us about 3:00 a.m. with the news. The person who first called 911 was passing over the bridge and saw Gina park her Land Rover at the top in the far right-hand lane heading downtown. He saw her get out and climb over the rail to the walking lane. Several witnesses have corroborated. The second call to 911 was a resident of the Renaissance, those condos on the Mt. Pleasant side of the bridge. They'd seen a person jump. This was all around 2:00 a.m. The police found the keys in the ignition and a suicide note on the dashboard."

"What did the note say?"

"*I'm sorry.* That's all it said. *I'm sorry. Love, Gina.*" The woodpecker was still pecking away.

"It was her handwriting?"

"One hundred percent."

"How did the police respond? Was there an investigation?"

"Of course. They did their due diligence. They talked to people. They figured out she had a history of mental illness. They put all the facts together and decided there was no foul play. Simple as that."

"I don't see how there could have been. Unless someone pushed her over, which sounds highly improbable."

"I know. I know." She put her hands on her lap. "Tell me *why*, then. There was a reason she was smiling in that picture. I told the detective in charge, but he dismissed it pretty quickly. Of course, he doesn't care why she killed herself, as long as no one else was involved."

"What reason?"

"She was in love. A week before, while we were trying on clothes at Hampden on King Street, I noticed a little sparkle. It was in her eyes and the way she walked and the way she talked, and I convinced her to admit it. You know how we all are when we find love. We can't help but bubble with life. I don't remember her looking that giddy since she was seven years old. Lord knows, she'd been a serial dater and a heartbreaker before I noticed that little sparkle. When I mentioned it to her, she admitted it to me but wouldn't tell me who he was."

"Why not?"

"Oh, I don't know. She was always one to keep things to herself. It was the first time in her life she'd felt that way. She probably didn't want to jinx it. She said she'd spill the beans soon. Anyway, I'm telling you this because I know she wasn't in one of her bad stages." Faye's smile faded. "So why would she do it? Why would my baby do it?"

Dewey stated the most obvious. "Maybe the person she had fallen in love with didn't feel the same way. Or maybe he or she broke up with her."

"Gina's not a lesbian, I can promise you that."

"I never rule out anything." Humoring her, he continued, "So maybe he broke up with her."

"Of course, I've thought of that."

They talked for a while longer, and Dewey asked for the keys to Gina's apartment, her cell phone, and a list of her family, friends, ex-boyfriends, and co-workers. He understood Faye's need to understand why. Over the past year, he'd spent many lonely nights wondering *why* himself. Why was he an alcoholic? Why had he done such terrible things to his family? Why did he have to drink? Why was he such a miserable person? Those answers might never come, but perhaps he could at least give this kind woman an answer to her *why*?

FAYE CALLAHAN DROVE off in her convertible BMW well after dark. Dewey decided he'd start first thing in the morning. He grabbed his mandolin from inside and went back out to the rocking chair. He tuned the instrument to the chirp of the crickets and picked around for a while, making up a few melodies and getting lost in the sounds of the night. He missed his band. He missed performing. He wished he had never let those guys down, but that was done. They'd never take him back. It was all too painful; those last few months when he was falling off stage and singing the wrong words or mumbling because even the wrong words wouldn't come out. At the peak of his collapse, he'd tried to stage dive. Not something bluegrass fans were accustomed to.

But he hadn't given up on playing. He was determined to get back to entertaining people. It was a major part of who he was, a part of his identity, and that was yet another hole in his life that needed plugging.

He fell asleep on the couch with the Big Book on his chest, the one he'd been introduced to at his first AA meeting. The thing now looked like it had been through hell, with its folded down pages and water spots and cigarette burns. In fact, it *had* been through hell, and he'd been the one carrying it through.

Despite all the shitty stuff hovering around his life, Dewey was feeling good as he pulled into downtown Charleston onto Bull Street the next morning. Damn good, in fact. Especially compared to the college kid with frizzy hair and unnecessary sunglasses making his way along the sidewalk, surely returning from an all-nighter of typical college debauchery.

Dewey remembered those days. He didn't miss hangovers one bit. Despite what he did to himself, his brain had come back to full service, and that was a darn miracle. He had been at the top of his class back in his high school and close to it at the College of Charleston, but all that drinking had worked away at his brain like a wrecking ball. He was thankful that he was able to recover. He liked his brain.

Bull Street was good living if you could get it. It ran all the way to the water on one end and right up to the College of Charleston campus on the other. Gina's place was in the middle, not too far from MUSC, the medical university. She had lived in one of the enormous century-old mansions that—because of escalating property taxes and dwindling trust funds—had been turned into funky apartment buildings that were perfect for the more well-to-do MUSC and C of C students.

Dewey walked down the long porch, passing two other apartment doors and some wicker furniture. He unlocked the door to 1-C and entered, closing the door and leaving behind the sounds of construction at the neighbor's house. He stood in the entryway for a moment. How strange and sad to be in the home of someone recently deceased. The family hadn't started packing up, which made sense considering they didn't even have a body to bury yet. Dewey had asked Faye to keep things as they were until he had found her answer, so hopefully any intentions they had were now on hold.

The apartment looked like Gina had gone to class and would be back any minute. There were dishes in the sink and cold coffee in the pot. But it wasn't dirty at all, especially not for someone her age. It actually looked like she had a housekeeper. The wood floors had that extra sheen to them.

Two impressive watercolors of flowers hung on the wall. He was no expert, but both looked like originals and looked expensive. Dewey noticed a laptop on the desk and made a mental note to take that with him. A copy of *US Weekly* and *People* were on the coffee table. Trashy magazine reading was certainly a much better vice than the ones Dewey had chosen in the past.

The bedroom was also quite tidy, save the unmade bed. "Who slept in this bed with you, Gina?" he said out loud. "Just give me a little clue." Dewey had been rightfully accused of talking to himself over the years.

There was another flower painting above the bed. "Southern women love things to be pretty as a picture, don't they?" he said. He stared at a framed photograph of the Callahans on top of the dresser. Hammond was the father's name. He had a thinning head of gray hair that, according to Faye, had once been red. Dewey planned on looking more into him later. Dewey loved playing the Bird's Bay golf course, so he wasn't exactly a fan of the guy.

Dewey rummaged around for a while, searching drawers, cabinets, and closets, looking for anything that might shed some light. He was hoping he'd find a love letter or a pair of boxers or even a picture, but he had no such luck. Nothing that even *suggested* she was in a relationship—which made no sense.

Dewey decided he'd better go through the trash. Not his favorite part of finding answers, but certainly one that had helped him in the past. Many of those old apartments didn't have disposals, so it was a nasty business. Dewey got through what was in the kitchen without heaving, though. Then he went outside to go find the building's main trash. The trash cans were lined up near the side of the house. He looked inside. They were totally empty. The garbage men must have been by lately.

He lit up the first smoke of the day and looked around. Some students were headed to class. One of them was pushing along on one of those long skateboards that were becoming so popular. He figured he should talk to the neighbors and climbed back up the steps to the wrap-around porch. Just as he was about to knock, an idea came to him. It was a reach, but worth the effort. The dumpster for the construction site next door was only thirty feet or so from Gina's front door. Closer than her own building's trash cans.

"If you have something you want to hide," he said, "you don't throw it in your own trash. You find somewhere else to put it. Maybe...just maybe," he asked Gina, "you had the same thought.

Did you?" He crossed over into the neighbor's yard. The dumpster was in the driveway. A couple of workers were on the other side of the house and couldn't see him. He put his hands on the edge of the dumpster and hoisted himself up so he could see inside. He started looking closely, scanning for something out of place. It was full of scraps of wood and nail boxes and rebar and PVC pipe and everything else you could imagine, but he didn't see any domestic trash bags or anything else that appeared unusual. "Well, it was worth a shot," he whispered to himself.

Right as he started to turn away, he noticed a pink box. He looked closer. It was packaging he knew all too well. And it was certainly something that didn't have any business being in a construction site dumpster. He made sure the workers hadn't noticed him, then lifted himself up and climbed inside. Moving carefully, he snatched the box and climbed back out.

He might have just figured it all out.

4

Back in Gina's apartment, Dewey Moses put the box that read *First Response* on the counter. He and Erica had used the same kind for both of their girls. Two of the happiest moments of his life had been seeing the double lines that meant "positive." Dewey opened the box and dumped the contents onto the counter. There it was, a used pregnancy test. Guess what...the lucky girl was pregnant.

The chances that the test was Gina's were obviously quite slim. He guessed there were plenty of women who had to be discreet with pregnancy tests after they used them, so just about anyone with a vagina could have thrown that box into the dumpster. Maybe a friend of his could grab some fingerprints or DNA from the plastic. He put the test, a hairbrush for fingerprint/DNA comparison, and Gina's laptop in his attaché and left the apartment. The idea of Gina being pregnant made the whole deal much sadder.

An Asian woman was now sitting in one of the wicker chairs on the porch, her bare feet kicked up on a small table and her eyes focused on a book.

"What you reading?" Dewey asked.

She pulled away from the book and looked at him with gorgeous cinnamon eyes. Her looks derailed him for a moment, but Dewey kept his cool and waited for an answer. She showed him the cover and said, "*A Crown of Swords* by Robert Jordan."

"I know it well."

She grinned. "No, you don't."

"I've read them all. Fantasy is my thing. You know he lived not too far down the road, right?"

"I heard that. On Tradd Street."

"That's right." Dewey was impressed. She was on the seventh book of the *Wheel of Time* series, a feat in and of itself. At around one thousand pages each, you really had to put your heart into it. "The next one comes out soon," he said.

"Are they still as good?"

"Every bit. Don't listen to anyone who tells you different." Dewey smiled, keeping his eyes from wandering. There were some fine legs in his lower peripheral vision, but he wasn't going to let them come into focus. He was married, period.

She set her book down on the table and asked, "Were you a friend of Gina's?"

"No. I never met her. I'm helping the family clean up her affairs." The lies came out so easily these days. "Did you know her?"

"As neighbors do. We didn't spend any time together other than bumping into each other and having a quick chitchat. I'm a little older. Why do you ask?"

"She was dating someone, and he left a few things in her apartment." *And the lies keep coming!* "No one seems to know anything about him."

"I saw a few guys come and go over the year I've lived here but never met anyone."

"Were any of them older?"

She grinned. "What is 'older' these days?"

"Not you, rest assured. I just mean...anyone ten-plus years older than her."

"Not one that I saw. Except for her dad. He came over once a week or so."

Dewey stuck out his hand and introduced himself. She said her name was Candice, and they shook. She held onto his hand a little too long, and Dewey had to stifle a blush. Sometimes you meet people that you're automatically comfortable with. Like you were good friends in a past life, and in this one, you can bypass all the formalities. Candice was a case in point.

"What's on your bedside table?" she asked, finally letting go of his hand.

Dewey felt a moment of invasion before he realized what she was asking. "Oh, I'm halfway through *The Malazan Book of the Fallen* series by Steven Erikson."

"Sure. I've heard about them. Are they good?"

Dewey lit up. "*Are they good*? There's ten books and I'm reading them for the *second* time, so yeah, they're good. He reinvented the genre. You need to finish the *Wheel of Time* series, and then run, don't walk, to the store to get started with *Gardens of the Moon*. It will change you."

"Okay, you are as much of a geek as I am." She named several other epic fantasy series, and Dewey had read them all. She'd read her fair share too. He could count on one hand the women he'd met in his life—including his wife—who were fantasy buffs.

Dewey knew their connection was starting to lead to trouble, so he thought he'd wrap it up. "Anyway, I could talk all day about this stuff, but I have to run. Can I ask a favor?"

"Sure."

"If you see anyone come by, would you please give me a ring?"

"I can do that."

Dewey pulled out a pen and wrote down his name and

number in the small composition book he always kept in his pocket. He ripped out the page and handed it to her.

She touched his fingers, and it seemed intentional. "You should take my number down too," she said, with a cunning man-eater smile. "Just in case you're looking for another fantasy."

For reasons that Dewey couldn't figure out, women had been hitting on him ever since he'd gotten married, and it was getting worse lately. He'd turned into a magnet for strong, aggressive women. Didn't they see the ring?

Dewey took her number down and got out of there like he was running from a gator.

ASHTON WHIDBEY, Dewey's college roommate from back in the old days at the College of Charleston, welcomed Dewey into his office. They'd met working at the college radio station as freshmen and decided to move out to Folly Beach at the end of the school year, leaving the dorms for good. While Dewey double-majored in Philosophy and Music, Ashton dove into Computer Sciences, going on to start a website design company that had blown up. He now employed seventeen people, and their "shop," as Ashton called it, was on the upper end of King Street, which was developing at a rapid pace. Back four hundred years ago, when Dewey and Ashton were students, upper King was a wasteland where you could easily get mugged. Now, any fashionable woman could easily spend a thousand bucks at her pick of any of the hoity-toity boutiques. Well, okay. So they were still mugging people on upper King. The thieves were just better dressed.

Dewey handed Ashton a basket of his Cherokee Purples and said, "I brought payment. Need your help."

"Helping those in need is all the payment I require," Ashton said, standing up to greet him.

"Right, I'll take these back then."

"No sense in having to drag them back home." Ashton rubbed his little belly. "I'll find 'em a home." He took the basket and went back behind his desk. At six-two, Ashton towered over Dewey by four inches and rarely missed an opportunity to remind Dewey of this fact. Dewey, in return, would often comment on Ashton's protruding Adam's apple and lack of taste apropos all art.

This wasn't the first time Ashton had helped Dewey with some computer needs. Dewey had been doing unofficial detective work for almost as long as he'd been sober, and Ashton had been excited about helping him from the moment Dewey brought it up. It gave Ashton a break from his world of HTML, Flash, ExpressionEngine, and whatever else Dewey didn't understand. Where Dewey was into fantasy, Ashton loved comics, and this was his way of fighting evil. The two of them had definitely had their ups and downs, especially when Dewey's drinking had taken him off the rails, but Ashton was the kind of friend who would always be there and would always forgive. In exchange for Ashton's computer virtuosity, Dewey would bring him a basket of 'maters, the currency of Deweyland.

Ashton's office looked like a NASA control center, the only difference being that just about every piece of hardware had an Apple logo on it. Some dance music played quietly and annoyingly in the background. Dewey pulled Gina's Dell laptop out of the bag. Ashton snatched it out of his hands, flipped it open, and began to move through it like it was his own.

"The girl who jumped off the bridge Friday night. Gina Callahan. This is hers," Dewey said.

"No kidding! Let's do this." Ashton made no effort to suppress his excitement—though he was one of those guys who seemed thrilled and curious about everything in life. You could tell him about a visit to see a relative in a nursing home, and he'd listen with bug eyes and enthusiastic nods like you were telling him about the newest Batman movie. Dewey liked that about him.

With his Adam's apple bouncing around like a pinball, Ashton said, "You're getting the high-profile ones, now. What are we looking for?"

"I'm trying to figure out who she was dating. He left no traces, and no one seems to know who he is. Nothing on her phone. Nothing in her house."

"Oh, he can't hide from Ashton the Almighty. You know that. In this world, I am King. I am the light and the darkness, the lie and the truth. The thief and the law."

"Okay, I get it." Dewey sat and listened to the unnatural sounds of the dance music mix with the tapping of the keys as Ashton's fingers ran miles a minute. Dewey pondered the popularity of electronic music. To him, he found no soul, nothing organic. It was a lifeless mishmash of obvious pop melodies floating on top of a repetitive thump. Ah, to be a traditionalist in the modern world. Dewey wouldn't wish the burden upon his worst enemy.

Ashton finally spoke up. "There you are. Come to Papa, *Mamma mia!*" He kept working for a couple more minutes, making strange noises with his mouth. Then, "You bad girl. Shame on you, Gina. Gina, Gina, Gina." He made a *tsk tsk* sound. The printer started up.

"How long are you going to keep me in the dark?" Dewey asked, removing his fedora and leaning forward. "Anything of interest?"

"Only if you consider sexually explicit fetish games interesting." Ashton was speaking as fast as he'd been typing, and his Adam's apple was working overtime. "Looks like this *chica* had another Yahoo account and did a good job hiding it, but like I always tell you, once it's on a computer, you can't completely remove it. You can't run from Ashton. No, no, you can't." He turned toward the printer and retrieved the small stack of papers. He handed them to Dewey and said, "She had a friend who called himself 'Hungry Hippo' and he's a firs- class perv. There's some pretty hot stuff on here."

"Do I need to go to church before I read?"

"We should probably both go right now. My wife's not going to know what hit her tonight."

"Does she ever?"

"That's enough, shorty. You and I both know where all the sorority girls were while you were locked up in your room with your hands all over that tiny little guitar."

"It's a mandolin."

"Whatever."

Ashton made another remark, but Dewey had blocked him out and was now reading the e-mail exchanges. Gina had been writing this Hungry Hippo from a Yahoo address with the user-name Med Student. The notes were short but to the point. Extremely graphic and full of expletives. The common theme was that Hungry Hippo would pretend like he had certain illnesses, and it was up to the Med Student to cure him with sexual pleasures of the creative variety. From what Dewey had read so far, she was pretty good at it. Three weeks before, Hungry Hippo described having shortness of breath, lack of appetite, and heartburn. She assured him that receiving oral sex under a blanket on the beach in the dark would fix his problems. Seemed an awfully sandy procedure to Dewey, but he was no doctor.

"Other than spam," Ashton interrupted, "these are the only e-mails on the account. I left the login info in a Word document on the desktop."

"This is good work. You know what you're doing."

"You don't need to tell me that."

"Is there a way to figure out who Hungry Hippo is?"

"That's the thing with these large domain name e-mail

accounts. Probably not. Sorry, bud. I didn't read all of them, though...there might be something in there."

"This is a big help, Ashton. Thanks."

"My pleasure, Dewey Decimal System. I need to get back to work. You know where to find me."

Dewey walked back out onto King Street where the business-people were starting to look for a place to grab lunch. Dewey picked up a falafel pita to go and sat on the opened tailgate of his truck to eat. It was there on the back of that truck that he'd solved many a person's problems. After the pita, he struck a match, cupped it from the wind, and lit a Spirit. As people strolled by with their shopping bags and briefcases, his mind raced.

He still had some healthy leads: her father, her friends, her gym and the rock-climbing wall, but he needed things to happen quicker, before the trail went cold. It was obvious what he needed to do.

"What if I e-mail Hungry Hippo from Gina's account?" he asked himself. "Is that the move? I'll pretend I'm Gina and say that I survived the fall." Dewey smiled as he blew out a stream of smoke. "It could work, you crazy son of a bitch. It could work."

5

Back at his place, Dewey sank into the couch and began to comb through the e-mails, trying not to get excited as he looked for clues. (Excited about the case or about the specific content, you pick.)

He and Erica had filled the place with furniture from garage sales and thrift stores. She had dragged him up and down the road for months searching for the perfect pieces. Recycling furniture was part of the "green" side of Erica; she was kind of a hippie, without smelling like patchouli and having dreads. Of course he'd loved spending time with Erica, but Dewey had not loved furniture shopping, even when it was inexpensive furniture. Now, nothing would make him happier. As long as Erica was by his side, Dewey vowed he would furniture shop like it was his job.

A quick glance around the room could tell you a lot about the man Dewey Moses. An upright piano that he'd inherited from his grandmother stood to the left of the fireplace. His fiddle and mandolin rested on top. He'd been playing music since he was a boy, and they always said he was one of those who could play anything.

He was also an amateur geography buff, and there was a nice collection of globes on most of the flat surfaces. Erica was not that keen on filling their other house with his little obsession, so he'd always kept them at the cabin. There were some maps on the walls as well, including many that had been created for some of the fictional worlds of the fantasies he so loved to read. Middle-earth, Westeros, Malazan, and other places most would never know—or care—about. On the subject of fantasies, he also collected hard-covers of his favorite works. The bookshelf on the wall near the entrance to his bedroom overflowed with books by authors like Stephen Erikson, Robert Jordan, Glen Cook, Robin Hobb, and even Mervyn Peake.

Another of his hobbies was spread across the dining room table. He loved Euro board games and was currently playing one of his favorites, *Settlers of Catan,* created by the great Kraus Teuber in Germany. The game was only possible with multiple players, so he was playing as three different players, using three different strategies. Erica was the one who had gotten him into designer board games, and that was no doubt one of the first signs that Dewey had met his match. She could take him from time to time, and from what their mom had told him, now Sonya and Elizabeth were starting to show some skills.

There was no time for pastimes today, though. He needed to get into the minds of the Hungry Hippo and the Med Student. He dove into the e-mails. After a while, he was frustrated. They were very careful not to reveal anything that could link them back to reality. Other than a couple of mentions of a meeting (in an extremely vague fashion), the correspondence mostly consisted of this game they were playing.

Dewey did pick up one bit of information that he'd already suspected. The Hungry Hippo had mentioned his leg cramps, and she suggested thrusting himself into a younger woman from behind. So he was an older man. Perhaps nothing disgusting, just a few years older. And yes, it was apparently a man, as thrusting isn't exactly a lesbian maneuver.

The other e-mails with symptoms and diagnoses gave away nothing but were quite entertaining. The Hippo's head hurt, and she said the cure would involve covering both his "heads" in Vaseline and rubbing both of them in a clockwise motion until both came to fruition. Gina must have understood some black magic. Hippo was losing his hearing, and she recommended coming over immediately and banging her brains out. Dewey wondered what one had to do with the other, but again, he was no doctor or voodoo man. The Hungry Hippo's back was bothering him, and she said she knew of a massage parlor run by a naughty med student who "supposedly" gave happy endings with whipped cream.

And Dewey's favorite: the Hungry Hippo had taken too much Viagra, and he was having a hard time (yes, he used the word "hard") getting it to go down. The Med Student said she could suck the stiffness out of the Eiffel Tower if she wanted to and that ten minutes in her mouth would get things back to normal.

"Whatever happened to good ol' fashioned lovemaking?" Dewey asked himself. Feeling slightly dirty, he set the papers aside and set her computer on his lap. He got into her Yahoo account and started a new message. The closer he got to sending an e-mail, the more absurd it seemed. *Impersonating a dead woman.* That had to be a new low in his newly-found career. Still, you had to shake those trees.

With the subject, *I'm back,* Dewey wrote, *I'm alive. I need you now. Can we meet? I'll explain everything. Please, I'm begging you.*

That was to the point enough. Assuming this man had heard about her death, he'd be beyond shocked but perhaps curious. After all, they still hadn't found a body. Dewey hoped they didn't, for at least a little while longer.

"Check your e-mail, my friend," Dewey said. "That's what I need you to do. Just give me a fighting chance."

Dewey tended to his garden, making sure the irrigation system had done its job and then walked around talking to the plants, something he'd been doing ever since he'd moved out there. They were about all he had these days.

At 4:00 p.m., he packed up his mandolin and made his way to the rehab joint in West Ashley that had brought him back from the dead. It had been ninety long days bunking it up with twenty of the dirtiest, roughest, and saddest individuals he'd ever encountered, but he'd walked out a new man, and, for that, he owed the place his life. Every Wednesday, he returned for a meeting, and somehow, they'd talked him into bringing his mandolin this time to do some entertaining afterwards. Anything to take their minds off the fight.

He'd invited a banjoist named T.A. Reddick to join him. Reddick had just left the DEA, so he understood addiction. T.A. had gladly accepted, not knowing Dewey had another motive as well.

Twenty-four men and women, all addicts of varying degrees, sat in folding chairs under the shade of an oak tree behind the two-story brick house that had been turned into a rehab/halfway house by an older addict who had been sober for twenty-some-thing years. He had thrown a bunch of bunk beds into the bedrooms, six coffee makers into the kitchen, ashtrays on every stoop, and started inviting people. Dewey had heard about it at his first AA meeting, and it had done the trick.

It was Mexico hot, and Dewey's short sleeve button-down was showing perspiration. He'd put his fedora on the ground next to him. They all had the Big Book open in their laps, and more than half of them held burning cigarettes in their fingers, smoke rising into the air like lowcountry fog. After the Serenity Prayer, the experienced ones took turns reading and commenting. With a butt in between his fingers, Dewey read a bit about spirituality and talked about what it meant to him, how finding something to believe in had pulled him through. For Dewey, it was love. The love he felt for his family. He talked about Erica and Sonya and Elizabeth, and he wiped away tears as he spoke about the pain of not coming home to them every day.

A young woman, maybe twenty, took the spotlight next and told her story. She looked too young to be there, but there were always a few of those. She pulled at her necklace as she spoke of her alcoholism and getting kicked out of her house at sixteen, and having a child when she was seventeen with a drug addict who still didn't know she'd gotten pregnant. Not too long ago, she'd put a gun to her head. But before she pulled the trigger, her son walked in. It was at that moment that she woke up and realized that she couldn't leave him alone. She found an AA meeting and checked into rehab that day. And she was now seventy-one days sober. No eyes were dry by the time she finished.

T.A. Reddick pulled up in his old CJ7 Jeep as the meeting was finishing. Dewey asked for ten minutes and went over to say hello. The bluegrass world is a small one, and Dewey kept hearing T.A.'s name, but everyone said he never took the stage. Desperate for some musical companionship, Dewey had finally found someone who knew where T.A. lived and paid him a visit with a mandolin in his hand. T.A. invited him into his James Island home, they picked music on the dock overlooking the marsh late into the night, and a friendship began. That was five months ago.

T.A. hopped down from his Jeep in cowboy boots and jeans. Dewey had never seen him in anything else. The man was in good shape, built tough, but nothing was out of place and bulky. During their picking sessions, T.A. had shared stories of his life with the

DEA, and it was a wonder he was still alive. You could see the scars of rough living. He'd left that all behind, though, and was now living off an inheritance from his murdered father and some good money he was making from writing country songs for well-known Nashville artists.

"Thanks for coming." Dewey reached out and shook his hand.

"I'll play for anybody willing to listen, brutha." He pulled his banjo from the back. "How's your jumper case?"

"Jumper case?" Dewey asked.

"The girl who jumped."

"Oh, coming along. Actually, I have a favor to ask you." Dewey handed him a brown bag.

"What's this?"

"A pregnancy test and a hairbrush."

"I appreciate it. You saved me a trip to the store."

Dewey laughed. "Do you think you could find out if the test was used by the same person who owned the hairbrush? I'm sure there is DNA, if not prints. Do you still have connections?"

"I could probably make it happen."

"I'll trade you for a basket of my veggies and a big bag of those Cajun boiled peanuts you like."

"Give me a day."

Dewey and T.A. tuned up and played for those lost souls of addiction for more than an hour, and it made their audience damned happy. It made Dewey happy too. They both sang and played their asses off, performing like there were ten thousand people watching them, and as T.A. wrapped up the set with a "Shave and a Haircut" lick, Dewey looked at each one of those addicts with encouragement, hoping they would keep fighting the good fight. Keep fighting, keep hoping, and keep loving.

DEWEY GOT BACK to his place around seven, eager to find out if the Hungry Hippo had responded. Still in a bluegrass state of mind, he put on *Church Street Blues* and let Tony Rice get after it for a while.

With little hope, Dewey opened up Gina's computer. "I don't even know why you'd still be checking this e-mail unless you have some other women on the line. I guess I won't put that past you. It's a slippery slope, my friend."

He got to her account. The Hungry Hippo had replied. "How about that!" Dewey yelled. He clapped his hands. "How about that!"

6

The e-mail read: *Oh, my God, baby. Is this really you? What did you do? I'm so happy. Can we meet tomorrow at 11:00 a.m.? Same place as last week? I can't get away until then. Are you still in Charleston? Be careful.* He didn't sign his name.

Dewey read it several times. "How the hell am I going to figure out where you met the last time?" he asked. Dewey pulled a smoke from the deck of Spirits and put one in his mouth. No smoking inside but he liked to let one dangle sometimes. Without thinking much more about it, he replied to the e-mail in the affirmative, figuring he worked best under pressure. He now had fifteen hours to figure things out.

He pulled up Gina's calendar, thinking that was a good place to start. Maybe she had written the meeting spot down, though it was unlikely. Matter of fact, judging by what he'd heard about Gina—the way she'd floated through life, how she had never even tried to find a job—Dewey guessed she wasn't that organized or busy enough to need a calendar. He was right. The calendar had never been used.

He dialed Faye. She wasn't able to give him any leads, but she said she'd e-mail him Gina's credit and debit card statements for the past few months. Without wasting any time, he called Gina's best friend, Sandra Wyatt. He'd gotten her name and number from the list Faye had given him when they first discussed the case. A woman answered.

"Hi, my name is Bob Tooman," Dewey said, offering a fake name. He didn't want to leave a trail. "Is this Sandra?"

"Yes, it is."

"Gina's mom hired me to help settle her affairs, and she told me that you'd be happy to answer some questions. Is there any way I could meet you somewhere? It's nothing to be concerned about. I'm trying to return a few things to their rightful owners, make sure everyone is aware of her passing, that kind of thing. It'll just take a few minutes. I can come to you."

"Anything to help. I'm at Pearlz Oyster Bar with some friends."

Dewey promised he'd be there in thirty minutes and let her go. He could have asked the questions over the phone, but that would have been lazy detective work. It's always best to get in front of them. To let them see you're human—and to catch them in any lies.

DEWEY CALLED Sandra on his cell as he arrived at Pearlz, and she came out and met him. Sandra was a dark blonde with light blue eyes. A Louis Vuitton handbag hung from her shoulders, and a sign on her forehead said she was a former sorority girl through and through. Dewey had a love/hate with her kind. They took a seat outside at one of the empty wrought iron tables lined along East Bay. It was windy and warm, a nice combination.

"Thanks for meeting me," Dewey said. "I know this isn't easy to bring back up."

"No, it's not." She was sipping a Cosmo but appeared sober.

"Did it surprise you?"

"Yeah, absolutely. She didn't seem that broken up to me over anything. I know she had some problems in the past, but I thought they were over."

"How long have you known her?"

"We met at the College."

"The College of Charleston?"

She smiled. "Yes, the College of Knowledge. I guess this was... ten years ago. We were both Tri-Delts."

Ding! Ding! Yep, he was right. *Yo, ho, ho, a sorority life for me!* Dewey loved and hated sorority girls, especially Tri-Delts. His first broken heart was a Tri-Delt at the College of Charleston, back when Gina and Sandra were in diapers. This girl had ripped him apart, and he was still thinking about it.

A young man in a mustache approached the table and asked if Dewey wanted anything. Dewey almost said that he'd love a half-liter of vodka and a dozen oyster shooters, but he held his tongue and shook his head. Being at a bar surrounded by alcohol was not easy business for him, but that was part of the drill. He had to get used to being the only one without a drink in his hand.

Looking back at Sandra, he asked, "So you didn't pick up any sadness last time you two hung out?"

"Not at all. She was on top of the world." Sandra frowned. She suddenly seemed suspicious. "What does this have to do with cleaning up her affairs? What did you say your name was again?"

"Bob Tooman. These are standard questions. It helps if I understand things." This girl had read too many mysteries. "Do you know who Gina was seeing? I have some of his stuff I'd like to get back to him."

"Mrs. Callahan already asked me that."

Dewey tried a more sympathetic approach. "Sorry, I didn't know that. I haven't gotten much out of her. She's pretty torn up."

"Yeah, I know. She and Gina were really tight. Anyway, I don't know if she was seeing anyone. She hadn't told me about it. Could have been a one-night stand. It wouldn't have been the first. I'm sure the guy will show up if he really cares about his things."

"You're probably right." Dewey lit up a Spirit and blew the smoke off to the side. "I think Mrs. Callahan is hoping I might find some answers while I'm poking around. That's between you and me, of course. It's something that usually comes with the territory. You learn a lot about someone going through all their things and meeting their friends and family."

"I can imagine."

"When was the last time you saw her?" Dewey noticed her tensing up, and he knew he needed to back off the interrogation. "Did you get a chance to spend any quality time with her before she died?"

"We worked out together Thursday, the day before she...you know. She was supposed to come to dinner with a bunch of us to celebrate my birthday, but she said she couldn't. Even though she'd already promised me. That wasn't like her. And then she was dead. I guess she had already decided on killing herself, but it seemed weird to work out the day before."

"She didn't tell you why she was cancelling?"

"She is the queen of vague. She said something personal was going on and didn't elaborate. I called her a bitch and walked away." She took a deep breath. "That's the last thing I ever said to my best friend."

"That's tough." Dewey had an urge to argue with her and try to show that she had nothing to regret. People never know when someone is going to die, and arguments are a part of life. But Dewey held back, knowing that sometimes women just want to vent. Yes: Dewey, the Woman Whisperer. He encouraged the venting by saying, "If you could only take it back, right?"

"Yeah, exactly."

Good job, Dewey. Now go in for another question. "What time was it that y'all left the gym?"

She wiped her eyes. "We always go from seven to eight, just before I have to work."

As the tears began to fall, Dewey's success in getting anything more out of her dwindled. After about fifteen more minutes, he wished her well and hit the road.

DEWEY DROVE BACK over to Gina's. Candice was sitting on the porch just like last time, her legs kicked up on the table, her eyes on her book.

"Still hooked?" Dewey asked.

"Hey, there. Yes, I'm hooked badly."

Dewey kept walking to Gina's door, trying to indicate he was in a hurry. "No one came by?"

"Not that I've seen. Can I offer you a cup of tea?"

"No, thanks. I'm in a rush."

"What a shame," she said with disappointment.

Was she hitting on him? He dropped the key *twice* before finally getting it into the lock. Why hadn't they done that when he was young and single?

Making it inside unscathed, Dewey went straight to the trash can in the kitchen. He'd seen something that had stood out in his mind the last time. Trying not to inhale too much of the odors, he began digging. Finally, after several dry heaves, he pulled out a receipt from Common Ground, a coffee shop in Beaufort, South Carolina. It was time stamped at 11:32 a.m. the Thursday before, not too long after Gina had left the gym in Charleston. The day before she jumped. What most interested Dewey was that she'd bought *two* coffees.

He was building a theory in his head and her going to Beaufort fit into it nicely. Judging by the secretive nature of the relationship, it looked like she was sleeping with someone she shouldn't have been seeing. Was he married? Was he older? Was he high-profile? She hadn't even told her best friend about him. What else could it be? So they were having some kind of discreet affair, and they were meeting out-of-town. Beaufort made a lot of sense. It was a sleepy, romantic little town that was what Charleston was fifty years ago. The kind of place where you might have a nice sultry affair—as long as you were careful not to run into any other visitors from Charleston that you might know.

Dewey looked at his phone. Faye had sent Gina's financial statements. He ran through them, having to squint to see the numbers. What he found got him fired up, in a geeky, Sherlock kind of way. Two months earlier, Gina had bought something at a gift shop in Beaufort. Three weeks ago, she'd filled up at a gas station in Beaufort. Something special was down there. Dewey had no doubt that she'd rendezvoused with a lover there—most likely the Hippo—but was this where they'd met the last time?

Dewey went with it. They had to have met Thursday morning somewhere in between her leaving the gym and the coffee shop in Beaufort. They would have spent the evening together—an easy assumption after reading their racy correspondence—and then gone their separate ways Friday, where she went on to kill herself. This is where the guesswork came in. If they'd met in Charleston before the drive down, Dewey had no hope of finding out where by 11:00 a.m. He didn't even have a clue. They wouldn't have met at her house, he concluded. Hopefully, they wouldn't have risked leaving a car somewhere, and they had decided to drive separately. And that was *if* the Hippo was from Charleston.

There was enough evidence indicating they'd met down in Beaufort to at least give it a shot.

Dewey made small talk with Candice as he left but got out of there before things got too spicy. As he climbed into the truck with a butt dangling from his mouth, he looked at the picture of his wife and girls next to the speedometer. The three most beautiful human beings on the planet. He wasn't interested in anything else.

7

D ewey got up early the next morning and hit the road. He'd almost driven down the night before but decided to save the money on a hotel. Beaufort was about an hour-and-a-half drive from downtown Charleston. Before driving into town, he stopped at the gas station that she'd been in a few weeks before. As he suspected, it was a futile attempt, and he continued on.

Timeless in its disposition, Beaufort only stole the good ideas from modernism like craft beer, local food sourcing, recycling, and good coffee houses. Otherwise, the town seemed unfit for cars and more hospitable to horse-drawn carriages that mosey up the streets carrying dapper men and done-up women to the local theater to watch *Porgy and Bess*.

Dewey parked on Bay Street and walked down a back alley into Common Ground, the coffee shop Gina had stopped in. He ordered the biggest coffee they had, and walked out the back. Coffee and cigarettes...the recovering alcoholic's lifeline. The back door opened up to the stunning waterfront park that pushed up to the bay. Perfectly manicured grass stretched for blocks, and the flowers along the borders were in bloom. The benches and swings were full of people staring out over the marsh grass to the water. Lighting up a butt, he sat on a concrete wall circling a tree and assessed his surroundings. "I'm onto you...I can feel it."

He ran through the events of the Thursday before, the day they possibly met there. Gina and the Hippo had been at the coffee shop at 11:32 a.m. She'd left the gym at 8 a.m. Probably went home and cleaned up. Matter of fact, she probably spent a little more time than usual primping herself, preparing for her hot date. She had to pack, unless she'd done that the day before. "I bet you were out of your house by nine at the earliest, which would have put you here by ten-thirty. Not much time to do anything else. You either met in the park, in the coffee shop, or somewhere nearby. What to do? What to do?"

He walked back into the coffee shop and said hello to the barista. "Were you working last Thursday by chance?"

She thought about for a second and said, "Yep. Sure was."

He handed her the photo Faye had given him. "Do you happen to remember seeing her? She's my daughter."

She analyzed the photo. "No, sorry. I see so many people."

"Were you the only one working?"

"Yeah."

Dewey thanked her and walked out the other door toward town. He pulled out his iPhone. There were quite a few bed-and-breakfasts in Beaufort. Dewey put himself in the Hippo's shoes and said out loud, "You could rent a house, stay at a hotel or motel, or a bed-and-breakfast. I'd go B&B if I was romancing someone."

Dewey had brought Erica down to Beaufort a few times, and they'd stayed at a couple of the B&B's that came up on the Google map on Dewey's phone. First stop was the Beaufort Inn, which was a couple of blocks inland. Surrounded by gardens that had been host to countless weddings and debutante functions over the years, the Beaufort Inn was the quintessential antebellum mansion. It was painted pink in the great pastel traditions of the Caribbean, something that Beaufort and Charleston had taken as their own a couple hundred years before.

Dewey trudged up the steps, knowing perfectly well that getting info from someone at a B&B would be at least as—if not more—difficult than getting it from a hotel. The accommodations business followed strict rules in protecting the privacy of their clients. He'd learned that the hard way about six months earlier, while trying to find out if a man was cheating on his wife.

With his head held high and a certain air of confidence, Dewey straightened his plaid fedora and approached the young lady sitting behind the desk. "Good morning," he said. "That's a lovely brooch you're wearing."

She touched the dragonfly pin on her shirt and smiled. "Why, thank you. It was my mother's. How can I help you?"

Dewey handed the picture of Gina to her. "Did this woman stay here last week?" It was the good ol' honest approach.

The courteous and gentle smile of the young woman disappeared faster than butter in a hot pan. "I'm sorry. We don't share information regarding our guests."

Dewey took out his private investigator's license and showed it to her. "This is official business. She died last week, and I'm trying to find out about her last days."

She looked at the license. "You're a PI?"

With a bit of pride, Dewey responded, "Yes, I am."

"Why didn't you say so?"

"Oh, I thought I would just ask first."

"A private investigator. So you're not even a cop?"

Dewey visibly deflated. He was dealing with a smart aleck.

The young woman smiled dryly. "I'm sorry, but I certainly have no obligation to share private information with a PI. If you were a real law enforcement officer, I'd be obliged to, but alas…" She sat straight up. "You are not."

That was more than Dewey needed so early in the morning. A couple walked in the front door, breaking up the uncomfortable silence.

"Is there anything else I can do for you?" she asked, trying to move him along.

Trying the compassion angle, Dewey put his hands on the desk and said *sotto voce*, "Please. I'm trying to help this woman's mother find out why she died."

"Sir, we're finished here. If you wanted a little more respect, perhaps you should have gone to the Police Academy." She looked past him. "Next."

"You are a mean person," Dewey said. "Just a mean, mean person. And you've hurt my feelings." With that, Dewey turned and marched out of there.

He fired up a butt on the way down the steps, wondering what the heck had just happened. He had a knack for getting things out of people...but that woman was just born difficult. *You can't be fragile in this business, Dewey. Don't let her get you down.* Easier said than done.

He tried four more B&Bs to no avail. None of the staff was as mean, but they all were certainly equally unhelpful. Now it was quarter 'til eleven, and he hadn't gotten anywhere. His only strong lead was about to burn out. He went back to the center of town and found the clothing boutique where Gina had spent fifty bucks two months before. No luck. He popped into other stores, showing her picture and flexing his charm. After a couple more clothing boutiques, a stationery store, two antique shops, and a bookstore, he started to lose hope.

At a little after eleven, he swung by his truck, grabbed his camera, and returned to his seat on the concrete wall in the water-front park by the coffee shop. It was even more crowded than before. With no other options, he began shooting people with his Canon

Rebel and zoom lens. For thirty minutes, he shot photos of any male over ten years old that entered the park alone. He continued back on Bay Street, shooting any potential Hippos. Dewey Moses was on a safari. No one stood out, but that was okay. Maybe Faye or Sandra or another of Gina's friends or family would recognize someone.

A church bell chimed at noon, and Dewey decided to grab a bite. He cut through a side street heading toward Wren, his favorite restaurant in town. He was singing a song T.A. Reddick, his banjo-picking friend had written, when, suddenly, something crossed his field of vision in a blur, and he felt a loop settle around his neck. Seconds later, he was being pulled backward by what he later figured was a belt into an empty doorway.

The attacker threw Dewey to the ground and fell on top of him, pulling the belt tighter. He was much stronger than Dewey and cut off his air with ease. Dewey tried to roll away, but the attacker only pulled tighter and pushed a knee harder into Dewey's back.

It didn't take long for him to feel dizzy and faint, and reality momentarily faded away.

WHEN HE CAME TO, he was drooling blood onto the pavement below him. He gasped deeply for air, spending thirty seconds trying to calm his breathing.

He turned slowly, feeling the pain from where the belt had been. He brushed off bits of gravel and slowly pushed himself up. No one had noticed him. The attacker was gone. Dewey stumbled some before finding his balance. He dusted off his fedora and placed it on his head.

His camera bag was gone. He'd spent more than a thousand bucks on that camera and lens. What a bad day. His wallet was missing too, although the man hadn't taken his phone or his smokes.

Dewey was tempted to call the cops, but to what end? They always slowed him down. Dewey was clearly on the right track. Had he taken a picture of this attacker earlier? Most likely.

His throat still felt a bit raw, but his head was clear; luckily, it didn't seem like he had gotten any kind of a concussion when he hit the ground. Dewey decided he was okay to drive. He stumbled to his truck and drove back to John's Island, defeated. To add to the misery, the front door to his place was wide open. Someone had broken in. He ran up the stairs, saying, "No, no, no, no."

Gina's computer was missing. After a few minutes, he confirmed that was the only thing taken. It wasn't worth involving the cops.

After cleaning up his face, Dewey plopped down in a rocking chair on the porch. "This just sucks." The thing that bothered him the worst was losing his driver's license. He was not a fan of the freaking DMV. He'd almost rather start bicycling around, but then he'd have no way to transport his crops.

Dewey's phone rang. T.A. Reddick popped up on his caller ID. "Dewey here."

"I got your tests back, buddy. The fingerprints are a match."

"I thought so. Thanks for your help."

"You sound flat. What's going on?"

"Having a less than stellar day, that's all." Dewey elaborated.

"Let me know if you need a professional's help. You PI's love to get in over your heads."

"Why is everybody a PI hater these days?"

"You people are a dime a dozen, Dewey Moses. A dime a dozen. And at least half—you not included—are numbskulls."

"Anyway, let me go before I kill myself. Hopefully we can get together and pick some tunes soon."

"I look forward to it."

Dewey made a sandwich and sat down with one leg over the other to read the day's paper. On the second page of the *Post and Courier*, something caught his attention. The headline read, "Golfers, Say Good-bye to Bird's Bay." There was a picture of two men underneath. The man on the left, the older of the two, was Hammond Callahan, Gina's father.

The man on the right, as captioned beneath, was Rowe Tinsley. Dewey didn't recognize the name, but he certainly recognized the face. "Where have I seen you before?" he said, setting the open paper down on his lap and taking a bite of the sandwich.

He looked back down at the photo. The man looked to be around Dewey's age—just under the hill. He was celebrity handsome and had a confident half-smile that showed he knew it. His hair was cut very short and showed some graying around the ears.

Dewey enjoyed another bite without taking his eyes off the photo. It was the gray sideburns that finally triggered the memory. He sat up and jabbed his finger at the man's head. "It was early today! In the park!"

In fact, Dewey had taken a picture of him. Rowe Tinsley had been walking alone in the park, wearing suit pants and a white button-down. It looked like he'd just taken off his tie.

Dewey's day just got a lot better.

8

"Rowe Tinsley. Are you my guy?" Dewey stared long and hard at the man in the photo. "I bet you didn't count on me having a photographic memory. I'm going to get you, you little dirt eater."

Dewey read the article. Over the past two months, he had read several like it, discussing the details of Bird's Bay and its possible development into a luxury community with stand-alone homes, condos, parks, a marina, and retail and restaurant spaces. Dewey had a vested interest, as he loved the game of golf and had been playing since he was four. Matter of fact, he'd been playing Bird's Bay for more than thirty years. Dewey played in high school but didn't bother with the College team. He liked to think he could have made it. Though his size kept him from being a big hitter, his short game was top-notch. Or at least it used to be.

He didn't get out as much as he used to, but when he did, Bird's Bay was high on the list. It was the best inexpensive course in the state. Many of the holes were right on the harbor. Not to mention, it was the closest course to downtown Charleston, so it was easily the most popular. He understood how controversial ripping it up could be.

Rowe Tinsley, the article stated, was Hammond Callahan's right-hand man at Brightside Development. With some very slick maneuvering, Brightside had managed to convince the state to move the public golf course to another piece of land. Since 1958, Bird's Bay had been owned by the people of South Carolina. The terms created at the time did not allow for the property to ever be sold or developed save one condition: a land swap. Supposedly, the written terms were quite vague when it came to the swap, but if a property of equal or greater value was swapped for Bird's Bay, it could be allowed.

A year before, Brightside Development, with the help of several sizeable investors, had purchased 284 acres north of Mt. Pleasant, off Highway 17. They'd agreed to build a brand-new golf course and swap the entire property for the land hosting the golf course and bird sanctuary on Bird's Bay. The state would keep the land, along with the water associated with the retired battleship. The reason the state was about to agree was because of that battleship. The Navy had publicly and formally requested a much-needed renovation of the ship, which had become a mainstay and serious tourist attraction for Charleston County.

The renovations were estimated to cost upwards of one hundred million dollars, an amount the state could never pay back based on the current income of the battleship tourism and the golf course. Brightside Development and its investors, as part of the land swap deal, had agreed to absorb half the cost of the renovations. As Hammond was quoted as saying halfway down the article, "We all win. We get to keep our battleship, we get a newer and better golf course, and we get to realize the true potential of some of the finest land in the Southeast."

"Spoken like a politician," Dewey said, sticking the last bite of the sandwich in his mouth.

He took a pair of scissors out of the kitchen drawer and cut out the article. Then he called Faye. She said she could meet him at six in Mt. Pleasant. He wrapped up a few things around the house and left a few minutes early. On the way, he called Ashton, the computer whiz, and asked him to put together a packet on Rowe Tinsley.

Getting to Mt. Pleasant required using several bridges. First, he crossed the John's Island Connector to James Island, then the James Island Connector to Charleston, then finally the Cooper River Bridge to Mt. Pleasant. Up and down and up and down and up and down.

That last bridge was the one that Gina had jumped off. Dewey had time to kill, so he parked on the Mt. Pleasant side and started walking up. The Cooper River Bridge was a three-mile long cable-stayed bridge reaching high enough into the air to let the thousands of container ships pass underneath yearly. It also reached high enough to provide for an almost perfect suicide jump. There had been ten jumpers since the bridge had been completed in 2005. No one had survived. Two had lived long enough to make it to the hospital but had died within twelve hours.

Dewey visited his dark side for a moment as he slowly meandered up the walled-off pedestrian path. He contemplated how suicide could happen. Even at the darkest of his moments, he hadn't given it much thought. And there were three reasons why: Erica, Elizabeth, and Sonya. He could never have left them. Even after Erica had kicked him out, when he was drinking two gallons of Russian firewater a day and barely eating and waking up not knowing where he was. Sure, he hated himself; sure, he didn't want to be alive...but the love he had for his family was too deep and unshakeable. He *had* to stay alive. He had to be there for his little girls, even if that meant only sending them love from afar.

Dewey thought about the woman he'd heard speak at the AA meeting. It was her little boy who had saved her. He was the reason she couldn't do it. If you had nothing to live for, killing yourself might not be that difficult, but for someone with a child—even one in your belly—it really wasn't an option. So Dewey was having a hard time accepting the fact that Gina had jumped over that bridge on her own.

"Did someone make you do it?" he asked. "What did Rowe, the Hippo, have to do with it? Did he really break your heart so badly that you wanted to take his child away from him? *Your* child? It makes no sense to me."

Dewey looked at the bikers and joggers and walkers enjoying the beautiful late afternoon. The view from up there was hard to beat. Charleston truly was a city of wonder. As he looked over the low skyline of Charleston, Dewey thought about how it probably didn't look that much different than it had eighty years ago. The powers that be, the South-of-Broad folks—the same ones who were pushing for the Bird's Bay development and more disastrous cruise business (an entirely different discussion)—had done one thing really well, and that was preserving their precious Holy City. It was nothing short of the finest place on earth to Dewey. He was never going anywhere. The ocean, the food, the scenery, the people, the fertile soil. What else do you need?

Reaching the top, Dewey took hold of the rail and looked down. His legs tingled. Yes, sir, it was a long way down. The boats looked miniscule from up there, but the harbor looked massive and dangerous and deadly. He wasn't particularly fond of heights, so he couldn't imagine jumping.

Something occurred to Dewey. "But you weren't afraid of heights, were you, Gina? This was like just another day at the wall."

～

DEWEY MET Faye about fifteen minutes later in the Whole Foods parking lot. She climbed into his truck. Despite everything in his life being a mess, Dewey was a clean guy, and this included the inside of his truck. They shook hands, exchanged pleasantries, and she commented on his cleanliness. He told her it was from his OCD military grandfather having raised him.

Wasting no more time, Dewey handed Faye the newspaper clipping of her husband and the potential Hippo. "I'm assuming you know Rowe Tinsley pretty well?"

"Sure, I know Rowe. What does he have to do with this?"

"Potentially everything." He explained what led him to Beaufort and what happened there. Then he dropped the bomb. "Rowe was there in the park. He was one of the men I took a picture of."

"You're sure?"

"Positive. Is this a possibility?"

She stared off through the windshield. A painful minute later, she said, "I hate him. I hate Rowe. He's a playboy. Yes, it's a possibility. Hammond will kill him, literally."

"We can't make assumptions. It could very well be a coincidence."

"Well, I doubt it. This is exactly the kind of thing that that predator would do."

"Let me find out more before you get ahead of yourself. Please, Faye."

She nodded, still staring out. Dewey felt the phone in his pocket vibrate. Someone had texted; he'd check it later.

"Tell me about him."

She finally looked at Dewey. "He's a first-rate scumbag. His wife has caught him cheating before. Maybe more than once. He told Hammond all about it one day during a round of golf. I never liked him since the moment Hammond hired him, but of course Hammond cares more about drive and intelligence than plain old common sense and moral stature. I can't believe this. I just can't believe it." She spoke with deep pain.

"Gina and Rowe knew each other?" he asked.

"Of course. He's been working with Hammond for more than ten years now. He's been to our house many times. And vice versa. We've eaten Thanksgiving dinner with them, for God's sake."

"Where does he live?"

"In the Old Village in Mt. Pleasant. On the water, near the Pitt Street Bridge." Dewey knew that area well. He asked her several more questions. Rowe's second and current wife was a stay-at-home mom to their twins. He had another son with his first wife; the boy was sixteen and a junior at Philips Exeter Academy in New Hampshire, one of the toughest preparatory schools in the nation to get into. (It wasn't just grades that got you in. This guy clearly had some friends in high places.) He was forty years old, about the same age as Dewey, so Rowe had had his first child much younger than Dewey had.

"There's something else, Faye." Dewey wasn't sure if sharing more was a good idea or not, but she was his employer. "Gina was pregnant."

"What?" Faye sat up and put her hands on her thighs. "What? How do you know?" He told her, and her kind face quickly melted into a ball of tears and sadness. Dewey let her work through it, suppressing a sadness of his own, and then said, "Faye, I have to say this—though I expect more from the two of you. If this does prove to be true, it's not a situation for you to deal with on your own. I told you I would find the truth, and I will, but I will not let the two of you do anything illegal. Especially your husband. You might want to think long and hard about even telling him."

Dewey offered Faye the handkerchief from his back pocket. She wiped away her tears and smiled in a deeply sad way. "Do I look like the kind of woman who would go break someone's legs for sleeping with my daughter? I'm sure he's not the first older man that she'd slept with. Or married one. But I can promise you that, if this is true, Rowe will certainly be looking for a new job within a week, and most likely a new wife. I'll make sure she finds out. That bastard."

Dewey was suddenly seeing the darker side of Faye Callahan, the apple-pie-baking, sweet mother of one. Of course, everyone has a dark side somewhere, and this news was enough to provoke the worst in anyone. Matter of fact, although he was telling her that he didn't condone any illegal activity, he was thinking how— had it been one of his daughters—he'd be feeling quite differently.

"You find out the truth, Dewey Moses," she told him. "You find out the truth, and you come tell me immediately. I want proof."

"I will. You're going to stay out of it, right? I can't have you going around telling people, especially Hammond."

"I will stay out of it until you confirm it."

"Good. I don't like Rowe any more than you. He whooped my butt this morning. But you're only going to slow me down if you don't listen to me."

She opened the car door. "I want to know if he was sleeping with my daughter and exactly what that had to do with her suicide. I know it had something to do with that baby. You find out if he's the reason my baby girl and my grandbaby are dead."

"Yes, ma'am. I'll be in touch."

As she closed the door, worry washed over Dewey. This was getting unhealthy. He did not get into this business to create more pain for people; he got into this business to solve people's problems. To do something good for somebody else for once in his life. At the moment, he didn't feel like he was helping anyone.

He'd intended on grabbing a quick lunch in Whole Foods, but he'd lost his appetite. Instead, he took a seat on the tailgate and fired up a smoke. After a couple of soothing drags, he pulled out his phone to look up the address of Brightside Development. No better time than now to go by and visit. Besides, Dewey wanted his darn camera and license back almost as much as he wanted the truth.

He'd forgotten that he'd missed a text message. It was from a number he didn't know. It read: *It's Candice. I live next to Gina. You told me to let you know if someone came by. Her dad's over here.* The text was followed by a smiley face emoticon. Dewey was not a fan of the emoticon. In fact, he detested them.

So Hammond was over at Gina's. Nothing wrong with that. It was probably a similarly cathartic experience to visiting a grave. Dewey had gotten everything he needed, so he wasn't worried about things getting moved around.

"Back to Rowe Tinsley," Dewey said, ignoring the woman passing him who looked entertained by him talking to himself. "I guess we need to talk." Dewey was not much of a fighter, so he wasn't looking to go another round with the guy. He did think about calling T.A. Reddick to help out, but he didn't. Non-violence was his method. Dewey was about to unleash some psychological revenge that would be much more satisfying than a punch in the face. Dewey was a peaceful man, but Rowe Tinsley had attacked him, and he'd cheated on his own wife. Rowe was not a good man, and he was about to pay.

9

Hammond Callahan looked in the mirror in Gina's bathroom. Her hairbrush and lotion and makeup were still on the sink. He looked at the wrinkles on his forehead and the bags under his eyes. His hairline was receding at a much quicker pace these days. The realization that he wasn't going to live forever was hitting him hard. He'd lived his entire life like he would live one thousand years, working harder than anyone else he knew, building a business and a name for himself.

For what? So that they would name a building after him after he was gone? Or a golf course or a development? Those things—the next deal, the next big payday—had mattered so much to him, for most of his life, but not so anymore. He'd never been there for Gina, and he'd never been there like he should have for Faye. That's what mattered now. Sure, they'd had a grand life, and he'd spoiled both of them to no end, but recently, that didn't feel like enough. What he had not given them was his time, the thing he valued most. Both of them had tried to tell him that. Faye had begged for it, but he hadn't listened. Not until it was too late.

And as it all came crashing down, he'd dug the hole deeper,

lying to Faye. He had to tell her now. He just didn't know how. She'd put up with him for so many years, but this would be the last straw. She would probably leave him. But he couldn't live this lie forever. He couldn't climb in bed next to his best friend for the next twenty years keeping such a secret. She needed to know what he knew. She needed to know why Gina killed herself.

The sound of the door opening in the living room brought him back. He pinched the bridge of his nose and inhaled deeply. How had it gotten to this?

He met Faye in the hallway, and she opened up her arms. "Oh, honey, come here." She could always read his face. They embraced, and he squeezed her tightly. How lucky he was. Somehow, she'd put up with him for thirty-eight years. She was the only one who had ever seen his human side. The only one who had ever seen him cry.

"I need to talk to you," he whispered, still holding her.

"Hold on. You need to know something." She pulled away from him. "I did something behind your back and I'm sorry for it, but I had to. I hired a private investigator to look into Gina's death." She looked up at him. "Please don't be mad at me. I know you wanted me to let it go, but I couldn't."

Hammond's stomach tightened. He remembered the conversation they'd had, when he had played it down, saying she needed to quit asking questions and let Gina go. He'd said it so she wouldn't end up finding out the truth and destroying everything. So how could he be mad at her now?

He took her hand. "I'm not mad."

"I found out who she was seeing, and you're not going to believe it...but I'm nearly positive."

"Who?" Hammond knew exactly what was coming.

"Your scum of the earth protégé, Rowe."

Hammond had already decided he wasn't going to lie about it, but this wasn't going to be pretty.

Faye continued, "Rowe Tinsley was having sex with our daughter, and he got her pregnant."

"*What?*" Hammond felt his heart jolt.

"She was pregnant. My PI found a positive pregnancy test with her prints on it. Your good-for-nothing protégé, the one you talk so highly of, is the devil."

Hammond was still trying to swallow this pregnancy news. Rowe hadn't mentioned that. What? The little shit thought he'd never find out?

"I want to know what you're going to do about it," Faye said. "You need to ruin his life."

"I—I already knew, Faye." It was the hardest confession he'd ever made.

"You *what?*"

Hammond knew the rest of his crumbling life was about to go right now. "I knew they were together."

Faye stiffened up and slapped him for the first time in their marriage. "You *knew?*"

"I couldn't tell you. I wanted to tell you, honey, believe me. But—"

"But *what?* You let it go on? What are you talking about?"

She started crying, and he tried to comfort her. "You get off me," she snapped.

"I didn't let it go on. I was on him the second I found out."

"And how did you find out? When was that?"

"I found out the day before she...the day before. I didn't want to tell you how. It doesn't matter how I found out. Please trust me—"

"*Trust* you? Hammond, you're telling me you knew our daughter was sleeping with Rowe, and you didn't tell me that little bit of information?" Her tears were moving non-stop. "Oh, my God."

"I didn't know she was pregnant. The minute I found out about them, I confronted him. That was Friday. I told him to end it."

"And decided to hide it from me."

"Yes. I guess I did. I didn't want you to feel any more pain. I was protecting you."

"Oh, you son of a bitch. You weren't protecting me. You were protecting your *investment*. Bird's Bay is what you were protecting. I've known you most of your life, Hammond Callahan. Don't even try to lie about that. You knew if word got out that Rowe was having an affair with your daughter, you would have lost investors. It was a simple as that, wasn't it?"

"That was part of it, of course. But the Bird's Bay deal is for both us. That's our retirement. It's the last deal I'll ever have to make. Do you really blame me for hiding it?"

"Yes, I blame you. I blame you for lying to me. I blame you for being such a shitty father that you'd drive her to pay you back by sleeping with Rowe. I blame you for her death."

"You don't mean that." Hammond felt broken.

Faye fell to her knees. "You killed my baby."

Hammond knelt and tried to put his arm around her.

"No! No!" She swatted at him as he covered his head. "Don't ever touch me again. You're an evil, selfish bastard!"

"I'm so sorry, honey. Please try to understand."

"I want a divorce."

"Hey, you're upset. Let's just calm down and talk about this."

Faye pushed herself up. "Never contact me again. You understand?"

"Faye, please."

"A lawyer will contact you."

This couldn't be happening. Hammond didn't know what to say. He choked up and began crying, begging for her forgiveness. He was crying her name even after she'd closed the door and left.

Hammond got up and stumbled into the living room. It was too much for him. Enraged, he lifted a floor lamp, yanked its cord from the wall, and began swinging it at anything and everything. He knocked several holes in the wall and then went after the television, crushing the screen. He kept going until he had nothing left.

Faye was right. He was a selfish bastard. But he could not agree that Gina's death was his fault. If anyone was to blame, it was Rowe Tinsley. He'd taken advantage of his precious girl. He'd gotten her pregnant.

It was all Hammond could do to swallow the news of their relationship. But he'd had to, in order to keep the Bird's Bay deal alive. Now, though, with Gina gone forever and Faye not much closer, the Bird's Bay thing didn't make a damned bit of difference. The only thing that mattered was making sure Rowe Tinsley paid for what he'd done.

Hammond had nothing left.

10

Dewey found a spot on Broad Street a block away from Brightside Development. A man sitting on a cooler was selling boiled peanuts on the sidewalk. Dewey bought a bag and found a bench to sit and enjoy them. He could shell a peanut faster than anyone he knew, and as he ripped through the bag, he mulled over what the heck he was going to do once he saw Rowe Tinsley. He wasn't going to beat the truth out of him, obviously. He wasn't going to accuse him publicly. He needed to get in, shake his hand, make sure the man was comfortable, and then blindside him to see how he reacted. That would be a start, and then Dewey could find proof from there.

He polished off half the bag and made way to his destination. As he was pushing open the door, his phone rang. He backed up and answered. "You got Dewey."

"Hey, it's Candice. Did you get my text?"

"Yes, thanks for letting me know."

"You wouldn't believe what just happened. I'm shaking."

Dewey perked up and turned around, heading back down the block toward the bench. "What?"

"Mrs. Callahan showed up about twenty minutes ago, and they got into it."

Dewey parked himself back on the bench, holding the phone to his ear with his shoulder. "Oh, no."

"I could hear all of it," Candice said. "They probably don't know that the wall between Gina's bedroom and my bathroom is paper-thin. Gina and I joked about it a couple of times. We could have a conversation with each other without raising our voices. I feel awful, but I couldn't help myself. I sat in the bathroom and listened to everything."

"Anything interesting?"

"I'd say so." Candice told Dewey what she'd heard.

Before she was done, Dewey was already jogging back to Brightside Development. "Is Hammond still there?" he asked her.

"No, he left five minutes ago."

"You're a big help. You have no idea."

"I thought you'd find it interesting. Now, what do I get in return? Dinner at the very least, right?"

"I'm flattered," he said, "but I'm married. Can I get a rain check for the next life?" Even as he said that, though, he knew he'd still be in love with his wife in the next. And the next. And the next after that.

"The next life it is. I hope we both come back as rabbits."

Dewey's eyes exploded. Women in their thirties sure were randy. "I'll see you soon. Thanks for the help."

"You know where to find me."

"Yes, I do." He hung up and jammed the phone into his pocket. "Yes, I do," he said to himself. "But I don't want you. I want my wife."

Dewey entered Brightside Development, and a cheery, bright-eyed brunette welcomed him. "What can I do for you?" she asked.

"I'm looking for Rowe Tinsley."

"You missed him by about an hour. He was going out into the

field and wasn't planning on coming back. Can I leave a message? Are you working with him?"

"No, no. Just an old friend. Do you have his cell number?"

"Sure." She wrote it on a yellow sticky note and handed it to him. He thanked her and went on his way.

Back in his truck, Dewey tried Rowe's number. He got his voice mail. Despite feeling like kicking the guy in the teeth, he didn't want anyone else to get hurt. He didn't leave a message, thinking it would be better to tell him in person. Then Dewey tried Faye. She didn't pick up, either. "I guess I'll go to Rowe's house," Dewey said. "Not sure what else I can do."

THE OLD VILLAGE of Mt. Pleasant tucked up against the harbor, and you could find some of the prettiest homes in Charleston there. It was an older neighborhood, with most of the houses built in the 1950s. Many of them had the same floor plans. As the property value rose, people began to tear down and rebuild, creating some appealing diversity.

The Charleston Harbor came into view as Dewey worked his way through the increasingly quieter streets. He hung a left onto Pitt Street and, after a couple of more turns, reached the Tinsley's waterfront address. It was a home that all parents wish they could raise their kids in. The rectangular yard was obnoxiously big for such desired real estate. Looking at it from the road, the house was on the right side of the property, and the green lawn stretched out on the left, along the harbor. There was a ring of chairs circling a fire pit near the water, and Dewey was sure there was a nice, big porch on the other side of the house. Rowe Tinsley drank his coffee in the morning overlooking Fort Sumter, where the Civil War began. Oh, what greed could get you.

The house was actually one of the older brick ones, but it

looked like it had been added onto a time or two since its ground-breaking in the fifties. The front door was turquoise, a nice touch.

There were a Mercedes SUV and Rowe's Jaguar in the U-shaped driveway. Rowe was home. Dewey continued to the end of the cul-de-sac and turned around. He stopped two houses away and got out, looking like he was admiring the view of the water. He lit a smoke and took it all in.

Coming from a place of non-judgment, Dewey wondered what kind of man Rowe Tinsley was. What had led him to cheat on his wife? Was he a bad person? A selfish one? Did he not love his wife? Did he not love his boys? Did he have an addiction to sex? He certainly had a hankering for some kinky stuff. Or was it something totally out of his control? What if his wife didn't love him? Perhaps she wasn't faithful, either. This job had trained Dewey to look at both sides of the story.

In Dewey's own marriage, Erica had done nothing but her best every day. She had supported him and lifted him up and believed in him from the day they met. She'd been faithful too, even when he hadn't deserved it.

Still, Dewey found little pity for Rowe Tinsley, and not just because he'd attacked him and nearly killed him. He had no pity for Rowe, just like he had no pity for himself. Rowe had made the decisions that had led to this day. Dewey had no idea what was going to happen, but he had a pretty good feeling that Rowe Tinsley was about to have a bad night. Maybe even the worst in his life.

Dewey heard some shouting and saw two boys run out into the backyard. Rowe Tinsley followed with a football in his hand, his arm cocked back as he encouraged his boys to run a route. Dewey watched them play for a while. Maybe he had a little pity for the man. Seeing a family broken apart was not something he would ever relish.

As Dewey stubbed out the butt, ripped the filter off, and stuck it in his pocket, he saw Hammond Callahan's Cadillac pull onto the street.

"This is not good," Dewey said to himself. "I was really hoping you weren't going to show up."

Dewey got back into his truck but didn't start the engine. Hammond parked behind the other expensive cars in the Tinsley driveway and knocked on the door. Rowe's wife answered. He kissed her on the cheek and followed her inside.

"Surely you wouldn't do anything with his family there, would you?" Dewey contemplated calling the police but decided against it. He wasn't sure what his role should be, but calling the police would only exacerbate the situation.

It went bad quickly.

Hammond entered the backyard ,and one of the boys threw him the football. He dropped it to the ground and pointed back toward the house. The boys went back inside, and Rowe and Hammond walked up to the water. An argument ensued and, within two minutes, Hammond drew a gun.

Dewey jumped out of his truck and started running toward the front of the house. Hammond had the gun pointed at Rowe's chest. Dewey placed a call to 911 as he tried to decide what to do. He wasn't the kind to carry a gun, so he didn't have much of a leg to stand on. The operator wanted him to stay on the line, but Dewey hung up.

As he reached the side of the house, staying low and taking cover, he could hear what they were saying. "My family is inside!" Rowe screamed. "Are you crazy?"

"What does it look like?" Hammond roared back. "You *made* me crazy. You took both my girls away from me. Both of them." His voice was cracked and depleted. "You got her pregnant. What kind of man are you? You killed my grandchild too. My only one."

"You're no saint, you bastard. It happened. I didn't know all this would happen. Gina wanted me to leave my wife and *marry* her!

She wanted me to help her raise the child. I told her I would help with the kid somehow, but I wasn't going to leave my wife. Don't tell me you've never ran around before."

"Not once in my life." Hammond looked very trigger-happy.

Wondering why the hell he was putting himself in danger, Dewey came around the corner and faced the two men.

"Hammond," Dewey said, the police are on the way. Drop the gun." How funny—sadistically speaking—to ask a man to drop his gun when the only weapon you have is your words.

Hammond swung the gun around. "Who the hell are you?"

"My name is Dewey Moses. Your wife hired me. I know she left you, but you can't do this. You will always have a second chance... unless you do this. Then it all goes away. Trust me, I've been there."

"You stay out of my life."

"I'm trying to help." Dewey decided that, even if the theory he'd been building in his head wasn't true, it was a good time to at least toss it out. Lies save lives sometimes.

Dewey said, "Your daughter is a—"

Right then, Rowe made a move. Hammond still had his gun pointed in Dewey's direction, but he sensed Rowe's movement and brought the gun back around and pulled the trigger. The shot rang out, but the bullet went too far right.

Dewey started running at the two men, both inches higher and many pounds heavier. Rowe's wife came out, screaming for everyone to stop.

Rowe tackled Hammond, and the gun fell off to the side. Dewey jumped into the fray, going for Hammond too. What Rowe and Dewey encountered in Hammond was a mixture of old-man strength and the power of anger. It was like wrestling something superhuman.

Rowe and Dewey worked together to pin Hammond down, but he threw several heavy elbows and kicks and pushed them off.

Then he rolled in the direction of the gun and was able to get his hand on it. Lying on his back, Hammond aimed at Rowe, who put his hands in the air.

He fired. Rowe's right shoulder jerked backwards as he grunted in pain.

Dewey wasn't done, though. He might have been small and inexperienced in combat, but he could be scrappy if he was forced to. He darted toward Hammond and kicked the gun with everything he had, and it went flying into the marsh with a splash. Hammond grabbed Dewey's leg and pulled him down. As he fell, Dewey threw a fist into Hammond's crotch that made him wail out in pain.

Dewey pushed himself up and stood over Hammond. "What I was *trying* to say, before you so rudely interrupted, was that I think your daughter is still alive."

Hammond let go of his midsection and looked up. "What? How do you know?"

Dewey heard cop cars pulling up. He said, "I'll have her come visit you in jail."

Hammond started crying.

Police officers swarmed the backyard, ordering the three men to the ground. Well, two of them already were. Dewey dropped onto his stomach close to Rowe. As an officer jumped on top of him and began to cuff him, he locked eyes with Rowe. "I want my camera and my license back."

Rowe stared blankly at him as a medic tried to stop the bleeding. "Is she really alive?"

Dewey wanted to say something heartless and cruel, but through Rowe's facial expression and the tone of his voice, Dewey could tell that he did care about Gina. So instead, he said, "There's a chance."

The officer jerked Dewey up by the arm and walked him to the police cruiser.

11

After the fight with Hammond and Rowe, Dewey hadn't been able to leave the Tinsley residence until 9:00 p.m. Luckily, T.A. Reddick had shown up and talked the police out of taking him in. Back at home, Dewey finally went through the e-mail packet Ashton had sent him on Rowe Tinsley. The Tinsleys had a second home in Beaufort, which made sense. One thing that kept bothering Dewey about an affair in Beaufort was its proximity to Charleston. Sure, it's a different town, but there's a chance you'll run into someone you know. It was too close. But not if it's at your vacation home. It's more private.

Or so Rowe had thought. He couldn't have been more wrong. Dewey found out much later in a conversation with Faye that one of Hammond's oldest friends lived right down the street from Rowe and happened to see Gina and Rowe drive into the neighborhood together. He thought it was odd, so he mentioned it to Hammond. That's how Hammond found out. He'd confronted Rowe the next day, and that's why Rowe ended it so abruptly.

Dewey hadn't bothered telling anyone but T.A. Reddick about his theory regarding Gina. Yes, he thought she was alive. Because a few things hadn't made sense. The first had occurred to Dewey when he heard the young mother speak at the AA meeting about her son. It was true: killing yourself was difficult, but killing yourself when you're responsible for someone else was nearly impossible. Even for those who were the worst off. Dewey couldn't see a young woman like Gina taking her child's life too, just because of heartache. What he *could* see was Gina faking it to prove a point. To see if she could break Rowe Tinsley's heart. To return the favor.

How could she possibly fake it? It had finally occurred to Dewey on the bridge. She was a rock climber. Heights weren't an issue. Maybe she'd used a rope. She could have lowered down, dropped into the water, and swam to shore. It was dangerous, but by no means impossible. Gina Callahan was in good shape. That was his theory. Gina was already unstable. Heartbreak can make the sanest person do things that are beyond the imagination.

THE TINSLEY HOUSE wasn't actually in Beaufort. It was on the other side of the bridge, two roads off of Sea Island Parkway, tucked back into the woods. Dewey shut his headlights off and pulled into the driveway. Flashes from a television illuminated the windows, and he had a moment of hope.

Well, it had been a crazy theory. Until he peeked into the window. Gina Callahan was lying on the couch watching a reality television show. Her belly wasn't even showing yet. She'd found the perfect place to hide out for a while. Dewey was a little surprised that Rowe hadn't discovered her while he was in Beaufort the day before, but Dewey figured Rowe had attacked him, stolen his camera, and then driven straight to John's Island to ransack Dewey's home, not bothering to go by his place in Beaufort at all.

Dewey tapped on the window, and she was on her feet in less

than a second and running down a hall. He walked around to the front door and knocked. "Gina, please let me in. Your mom sent me."

She didn't answer.

"Do you want me to call the cops? If you don't answer this door in five seconds, I'll call them. You're not in any trouble with me."

Dewey took out his phone and dialed a number. "Faye?"

"Yes?"

"This is Dewey."

She didn't say anything.

"Someone wants to talk to you. Hold on."

Dewey pulled the phone from his ear and knocked on the door again. "Let's go. I don't have all night. I will have the cops here in minutes."

The door cracked open. Gina was standing there in front of him in boxers and a T-shirt. Probably Rowe Tinsley's. Her red hair was in a ponytail.

Dewey handed her the phone. "Your mom wants to talk to you."

She put it to her ear. "Mom?"

Dewey heard Faye's voice explode with excitement as he turned and walked away. He'd done his job. They could work it out from there.

12

Dewey placed the ball on the tee on the first hole of the Bird's Bay Golf Course. He thought about how he'd saved this course, and he was happy about it. Sure, not many others knew that, but that was okay.

Shortly after the day it all went down, Rowe Tinsley's wife had a press conference and outlined the details of a slew of illegal activities regarding Bird's Bay. Apparently, Hammond and Rowe had paid several hundred thousand dollars in bribes to various state officials to facilitate the development. She'd overheard a phone conversation regarding something illegal and had taken it upon herself to investigate. She had more than enough proof.

The people of Charleston County went into an uproar, and the Governor of South Carolina had gotten involved. He was currently pushing through paperwork to permanently keep Bird's Bay as public land, promising that it would never be developed or swapped. No doubt he'd be remembered for it, and that's sometimes why we do the things we do.

No, Dewey hadn't cured cancer, but he had done a good thing for the people and for the environment. Yeah, this was good work, and Lord knows, there was plenty of it still left to do. He just needed to learn how to defend himself. Maybe even shoot a gun. His line of work had the potential to be dangerous from time to time.

Standing back from the ball, Dewey looked at T.A. Reddick, a man he had too much in common with to ignore as a friend. "When's the last time you played?"

T.A. pulled the sleeve off his driver. "I'm getting back into it as of two months ago. I quit for a while after a round at Wild Dunes years ago. The course and the wind ate me up, and I gave my clubs to the kid who was cleaning carts and left."

"What!"

"Yeah, I've got a little temper...that I'm learning how to control. Now that the DEA is out of my life, I finally have the time to clean up my game. New clubs, new game, new life...know what I mean?"

"I know exactly what you mean." Dewey addressed the ball and knocked it 270 yards down the center of the fairway.

"No breakfast ball today, huh?"

Dewey stretched out his arms, finally getting out of his finish. "Not today."

T.A. lined up and, without a practice swing, knocked the ball right down the middle, fifty yards past Dewey. T.A. had nice technique and an athlete's swing. Made sense; he'd told Dewey he played soccer for UVA.

Dewey said, "'Haven't played in a while'...yeah, right."

"I used to be good."

As they loaded their clubs into the golf cart, Dewey asked, "What else are you going to do with your time? You want to go into business together?"

"You mean make music, or this private eye stuff?"

"Why not both?"

T.A. laughed. "I'm doing just fine on my own."

"C'mon. Let's pick some bluegrass and solve a few crimes. I'll be the brains; you be the muscle."

T.A. laughed as he stepped into the golf cart. "Tell you what, let's make a bet. You beat me today, I'll start a band with you. I beat you, you deliver a basket of veggies to my door every week for a year. As far as the private investigation stuff, that's not my bag. You'll have to follow dudes to Motel 6 on your own."

What was it with people putting down his new profession? "Fair enough," Dewey said. "What should we call ourselves?"

"You really think you can beat me?"

Dewey stuck out his hand. "I'll take the bet."

They shook on it. Little did they know how much that handshake would mean.

Dewey knew he'd beat him—even after seeing that long drive. Because brains always beat brawn. Almost always.

After nine holes, Dewey was losing by six strokes, and it wasn't looking good, but he hadn't given up. He knew T.A.'s temper would come into play soon. At least, he hoped so.

What he didn't tell T.A. during the round was that today, Dewey was one year sober, and tonight, he was going to call his wife.

If you enjoyed my story, please consider leaving a review.

For free books, updates, and my occasional newsletter, please visit: benjaminblackmore.com

ABOUT THE AUTHOR

Benjamin Blackmore is a pen name for best-selling author Boo Walker. He initially tapped his creative muse as a songwriter and banjoist in Nashville before working his way west to Washington State, where he bought a gentleman's farm on the Yakima River. It was there amongst the grapevines and wine barrels that he fell in love with telling stories that now resonate with book clubs around the world. Rich with colorful characters and boundless soul, his novels will leave you with an open heart and a lifted spirit.

Always a wanderer, Boo currently lives in Cape Elizabeth, Maine with his wife and son. He also writes thrillers under the pen name Benjamin Blackmore. You can find him at boowalker.com and benjaminblackmore.com.

Made in the USA
Las Vegas, NV
19 August 2022

53634143R00052